# the company

SUNDIAL HOUSE

**SUNDIAL HOUSE EDITORIAL BOARD**

Anne Freeland

J. Bret Maney

Alberto Medina

Graciela Montaldo

João Nemi Neto

Rachel Price

Eunice Rodríguez Ferguson

Kirmen Uribe

verónica gerber bicecci

# the company

translated by **christina macsweeney**

epilogue by **cristina rivera garza**

2024 Verónica Gerber Bicecci

Copyright © 2024 Christina MacSweeney (English Translation)

Copyright © 2024 Cristina Rivera Garza (Epilogue)

The words and images in this book are a rewriting, thus sharing them does not constitute a crime. You can cross out, make amendments, or plagiarize creatively as long as you retain this note.

Cover design: Lisa Hamm
Book design: Lisa Hamm, based on the original concept
by Verónica Gerber Bicecci
Design consultant: Alexia Halteman
Editorial Assistants: Emily Oliveira and Liam Sebastián Ferguson
Publicity consultant: Avery Lozada

ISBN: 979-8-9879264-9-9

*La Compañía* "a." was originally shown as part of an installation titled *La máquina distópica* in the Museo de Arte Abstracto Manuel Felguérez (Zacatecas, Mexico), in the context of the XIII FEMSA Biennial: Nunca fuimos contemporáneos, curated by Daniel Garza Usabiaga and Willy Kautz, from October 2018 until February 2019.

SUNDIAL
HOUSE
*New York • Philadelphia*

*For Miguel Pablo*

a.

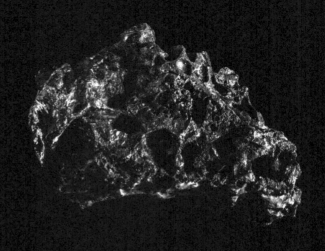

For The Company, you'll be something like a piece of furniture that one is used to seeing in a particular place, but which doesn't register on the mind.

You won't be able to stifle a cry of horror when you first see The Company. It is dour, sinister.

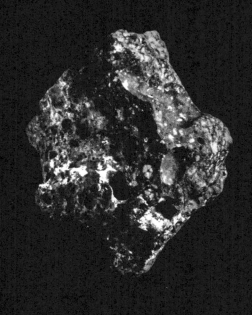

Its large, almost round, yellowish and unblinking eyes
will seem to pierce everything and everyone.

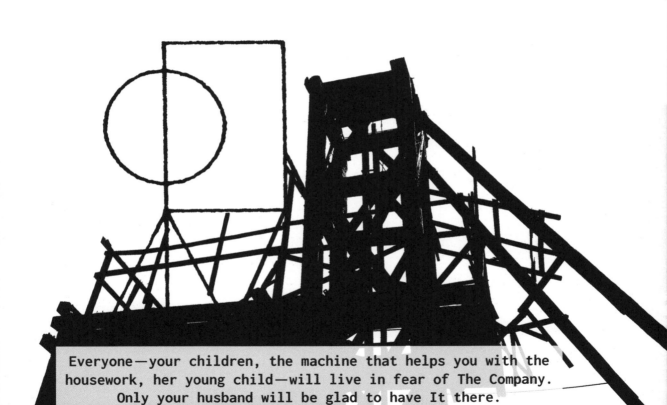

That first day, your husband will assign It the corner bedroom: a large room, but dark and damp, which is why it's never used.

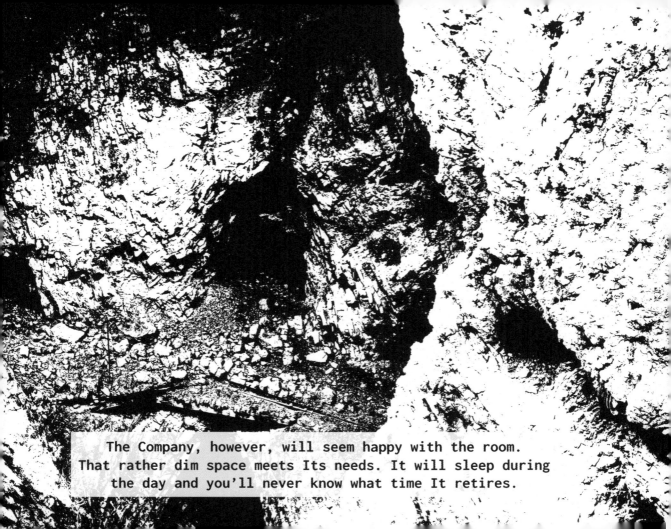

The Company, however, will seem happy with the room. That rather dim space meets Its needs. It will sleep during the day and you'll never know what time It retires.

The house will be very large, the rooms enclosing an interior garden.

Between those rooms and the garden, there will be a cloister that protects the inside of the house from the harshness of the wind and the arid soil.

The daily chore of cleaning such a big house and tending the garden will be hard work and will take up your whole morning. But you love your garden.

The cloister will be covered by vining plants that bloom throughout the greater part of the year.

In the garden, you'll grow chrysanthemums, pansies, alpine violets, begonias, and heliotropes.

The children will amuse themselves searching for caterpillars on the leaves. They will sometimes spend hours quietly focused on catching the drops of water leaking from the old hosepipe.

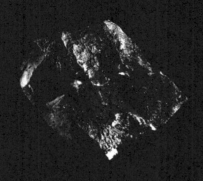

The Company will return to Its room
as if nothing has happened.

Once or twice, when you think It's asleep, you'll go to the kitchen to make a snack for the children and come across The Company in some dark corner of the cloister, standing underneath the climbing plants.

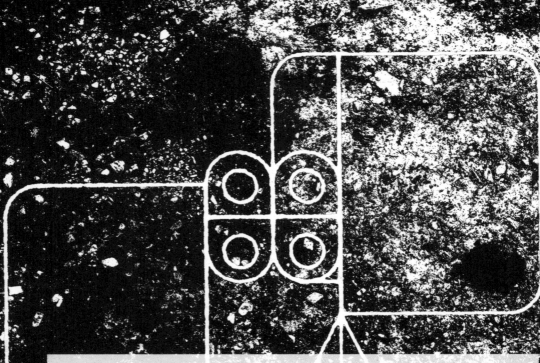

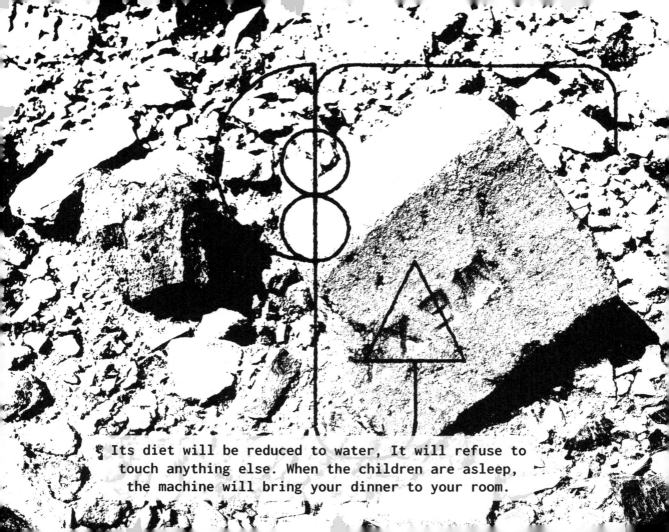

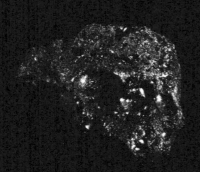

Since your bedroom door is always open, you won't dare sleep, afraid that The Company might enter at any time and attack you all.

On one occasion, he'll say that he has a lot of work on.
You'll think that he's found other sources of amusement.

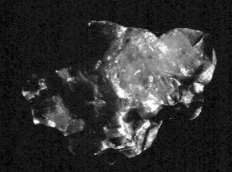

When you wake, you'll see The Company standing by your bed, Its piercing gaze fixed on you.

There's no electricity in the town and you won't be able to bear lying in the dark, knowing that at any moment...

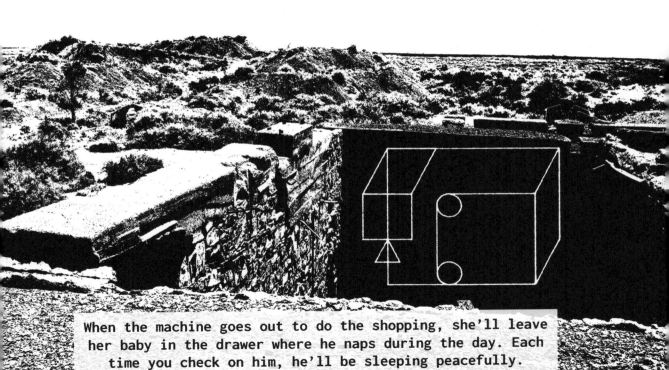

When the machine goes out to do the shopping, she'll leave her baby in the drawer where he naps during the day. Each time you check on him, he'll be sleeping peacefully.

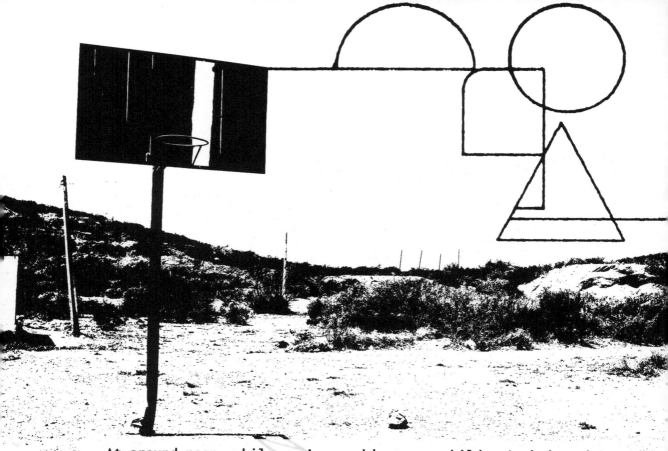

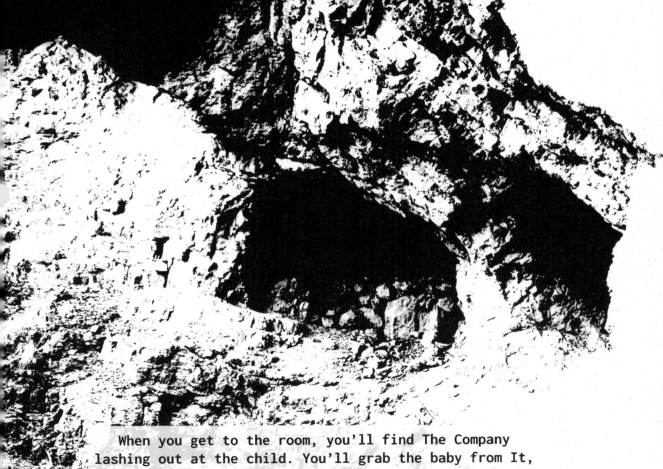

When you get to the room, you'll find The Company lashing out at the child. You'll grab the baby from It, although you'll have no idea how you manage it.

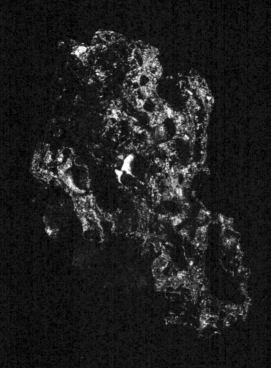

You'll rush at The Company with a bar that is suddenly in your hand and attack It in an explosion of long-suppressed rage. You won't know how badly you've hurt It as you'll have fallen in a faint.

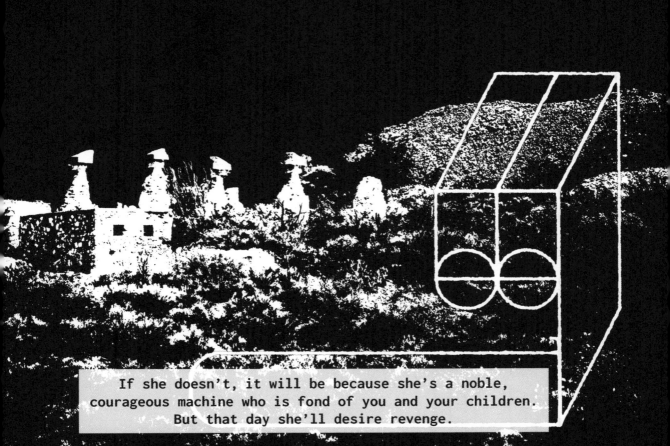

"You get more hysterical by the day. It's sad and depressing to see you like this. I've told you a thousand times: The Company's harmless."

Your children will be terrified; they'll refuse to play in the garden and will hang on to your apron strings the whole time. When the machine goes out to the market, you'll take them to your bedroom and close the door.

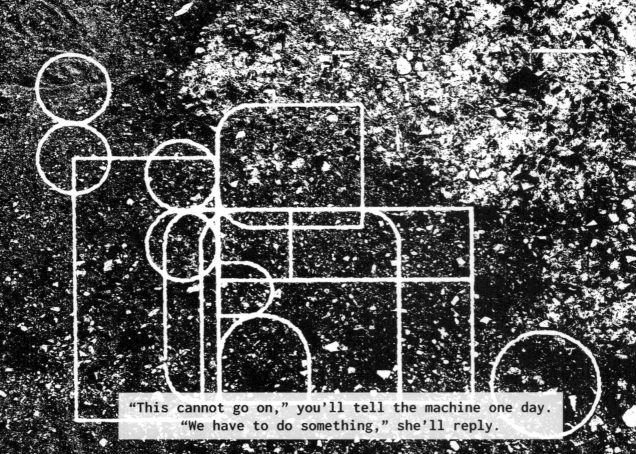

An opportunity will arise unexpectedly. Your husband's going to the city to transact some business. He'll be away for quite a while, he tells you, for about three weeks.

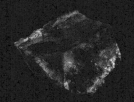

That day, The Company will get up earlier than usual
and stand outside your bedroom door.

From time to time, you'll hear The Company approaching the bedroom and then banging furiously on the door.

Hardly daring to breathe, you and the machine will pull the latches and lock the door. Then you'll nail the boards to the frame until the door is impassable.

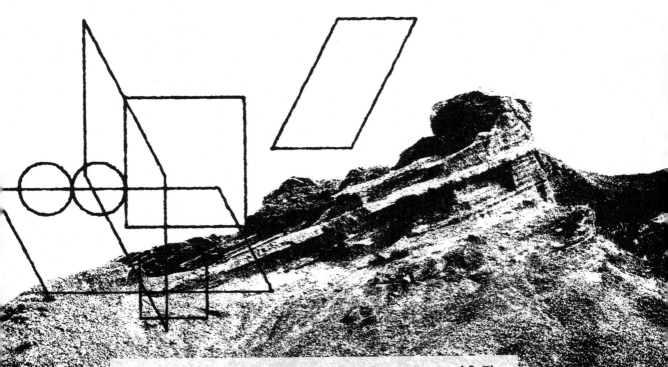

The following days will be terrifying. The Company will live for a long time, without air or food. Initially, It will beat on the door, hurl Itself against it, claw at the wood, call out in desperation.

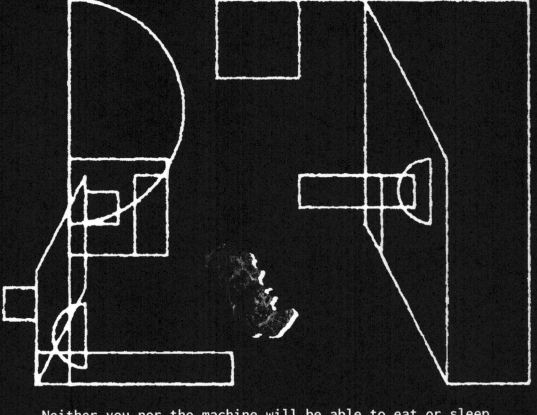

Neither you nor the machine will be able to eat or sleep.
The Company's cries are awful! Sometimes you'll worry that your husband might come home early. What if he finds It in that state?

The Company will hold out for two weeks until, finally, there will be no sound from the room. Not even a whimper. However, you'll wait two more days before opening the door.

b.

1.

San Felipe Nuevo Mercurio [is located] in the northeast of Zacatecas state (where, as they say, even the wall lizards carry water bottles), south of the impressive Pico de Teyra, in the foothills of the sierra. [There was nothing but a few] scattered watering holes and the miserable hovels of the farmhands....José Espinosa—tall, wiry, dark-skinned, hawk-nosed, with a straggly beard and an even thinner moustache—[was] popular among farmhands and the staff of the hacienda,...they used to call him "Long Tall José."

2.

Climate, vegetation, and hydrography: the climate of the region is mainly dry, tending to extremes, with high temperatures... reaching an average of 36°C from May to June. December and January are the coldest months, [with] temperatures falling below zero at high altitudes. The annual average is 16°C [with sparse] rainfall, averaging 510 mm. The vegetation is...chaparral, thorn bushes: prickly pears, fencepost and barrel cacti, palm trees.

3.

Physiography: The mining region of Nuevo Mercurio is located in the...province of the Sierra Madre Oriental, in the sub-province of Sierras Transversas.

4.

That week José had to go to San Marcos,...[to tend] the livestock.
...He noticed that all the bees [around the watering hole] flew
east, towards the Cerro del Calvo, about three kilometers away.
He [thought that] their hive must be on that side [of the watering
hole], and resolved to search for it the next day, because...that
would mean he'd have honey to take home, and his young'uns loved
honey.

5.

In mid-November, Eusebio Gaucín turned up. He'd come from
Fresnillo to look for mercury on his boss's orders....José
remembered that in his backpack he still had those red stones he'd
picked up when bringing the honeycomb back from Cerro del Calvo
and he shyly showed them....Eusebio examined [them and] licked
a part [of] one of the stones clean....He took out his knife,
scratched the rock with the...point and [then], looking pleased,
said, "Yes, it's cinnabar."

6.

The surface of Zacatecas is pitted with meteor impacts. Nuevo Mercurio was formed by one. The crater is hard to see now, but it still exists....Around the mines, there's meteorite material that fell from the sky millions of years ago. The mercury they extract from the place is from a meteorite that smashed into the earth and melted.

7.

8.

Cinnabar is the mineral [from which] metallic mercury [is extracted]. In the past, ground cinnabar used to be sold in packets in hardware stores as [the pigment] vermilion...."Look José," said Eusebio, "if there's enough of this mineral in the place [you're talking about], I swear on my mother's grave that I'll lift you out of poverty." That same morning, after loading...poncho, backpack, and [the] indispensable cask of water, they set off.

9.

The first recorded mention of mercury was by Aristotle in the fourth century B.C., when it was used in religious ceremonies. In the first century, Kioscorides Pedanius and Pliny used mercury as a medicinal ointment. From the sixth century on, the Egyptians frequently mentioned mercury, its uses and preparations, as well as tin and copper amalgams.

10.

They didn't have to dig...the rocks were littering the crest. They filled the large ixtle sack José was carrying....Then they smoked a cigarette apiece. Eusebio looked well content and said, "Now, José, I think this stuff is good. I want you to come with me to Saín Alto to talk to my boss. He's a man of his word and will reward you well." [In] Cañitas, where the Durango line...with the Mexico-Juarez, they bought gas at the railroad station and then continued through the night to Saín. After breakfast the next morning, they took the mineral samples [to] Don Nacho.

11.

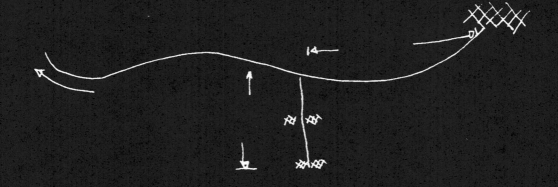

12.

Eusebio...broke up the [cinnabar] in the ixtle sack....They weighed out 65 kilos and added 10% lime. They fired up the...retort loaded with the samples. After lunch, at around four in the afternoon, they checked the result [of the test]. [In] the flask where the liquid had deposited [there were] 17 kilos of mercury, from which they calculated an ore grade of 20%. Fortune was smiling on José: Don Nacho offered both him and Eusebio a 10% share [of the business].

13.

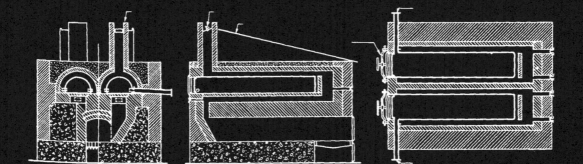

14.

Some say it was Sr. [Long Tall] José Espinosa, others [that it was] Aurelio Herrera who, between...1935 and 1936, discovered the outcrop that led to the opening of the mercury mine....News ...that the...site held a rich seam of cinnabar with a high mercury content spread like wildfire through the region.

15.

Discovered in 1940, [Nuevo Mercurio] was the most productive mercury district in Mexico, and one of the most productive in the Western Hemisphere, with a monthly production that averaged 600 flasks or more and at times exceeded 1,000 flasks. At Nuevo Mercurio there were 16 principal mines, about 50 smaller ones, and approximately 200 prospects.

16.

[Nowadays] San Felipe Nuevo Mercurio has electricity, [a very] little water, a telephone box, general stores for basic products, ...paved roads, tracks and paths that are passable all year round, telecommunications and telephone connections [although the signal is poor], [and] a 34 KV power line.

17.

Don Nacho, compass [in hand], took the exact coordinates of the site and noted all the data needed for his claim. By eight in the morning, his secretary was [already] filling in the forms for...a [mining] license and another for prospecting [rights]. The mining license covered the whole of the eastern side of the Cerro del Calvo. They named [the area] Nuevo Mercurio, and the mine, which covered nine hectares, they called El Engaño. The register was signed by Don Nacho and the mining agent, who then handed over the officially stamped documents. It was all arranged. Fifteen minutes later, other people arrived at the mining agency with the same [objective], and on discovering that they couldn't [stake a claim on] that land, they filed claims to [lots] adjoining Nuevo Mercurio: to the east...the Medinilla brothers with El Coyote and La Peñita; to the west of the El Calvo foothills, El Rosicler and, to the south, San José, which was [the property of] Sr. Juan Jiménez.

18.

Structure and extent of the deposits: In this district [there is] a series of mines along [an] anticline....The most important are San Pablo, San Isidoro, Los Tajos, Tiro General, San José, and La Cola, where the main seams are located. They range from 1 to 1.5 m in width by 500 m in length and are dozens of meters deep.

19.
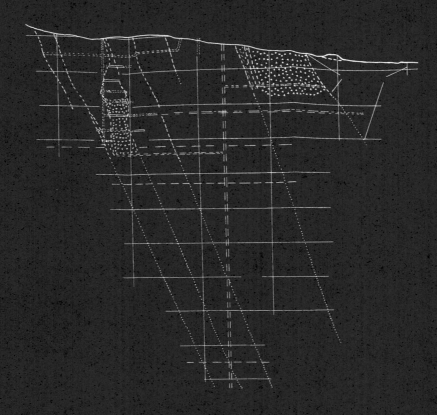

20.

The first business belonged to Sr. Ignacio Martínez under the name Mercurio Mexicano. [It was opened] on...May 5, 1940,...They originally...mined the rock face, following the mineralization.... Lack of capital and experienced miners considerably delayed the early development of Tiro San Isidro.

21.

Nuevo Mercurio soon [became the home of] miners who travelled there in search of work from a wide variety of places, including Parra, Zacatecas, Concepción del Oro, and Guanajuato. Cantinas and pool halls appeared, and a red light zone of wooden shacks... sprang up on the outskirts of the small town. It was...easier to get a beer than a glass of water....[Water] was brought from Cañitas [in] railroad water wagons to the station in Opal, 24 km [from the mine]. From Opal to Nuevo Mercurio, it was transported in tank trucks.

22.

As far as I can remember, the first death was up there in the Veta Rica mineshaft and the [second] was in the San José [mineshaft]. Those are the names of sections of the mine. Every section [of a mine] has a name.

23.

The Company was paying for the construction of an office for the authorities and a [prison] annex, both adobe buildings; the prison was sorely needed because the only cell available for the drunks and criminals was a seven-meter deep hole that the Company had dug when [it was] excavating the site.

24.

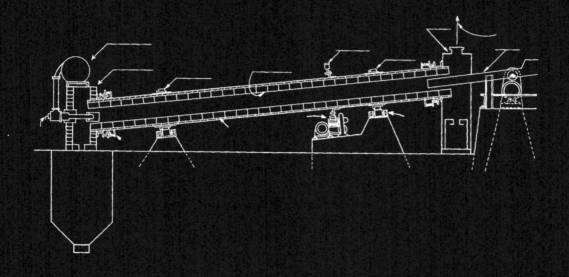

25.

Eusebio took on the task of showing the visiting engineers and geologists around the installations and the work in progress when...came to make enquiries. [He used to] eavesdrop on their conversations and their [use of] technical words...about the type of mineralization...of the deposit. [They said] it was most likely a hydrothermal deposit, [and he used to] repeat that information at the drop of a hat, which earned him the nickname "Eusothermal."

26.

The region is characterized by sedimentary anticlines and synclines dating from the Cretaceous Period. Within those folds [there are] deposits of metallic minerals...of hydrothermal origin that are principally associated with the mineralization of mercury and, at greater depths, silver, lead, zinc, gold, copper, and cadmium....[There are] also non-metallic deposits, including calcite, onyx, and marble.

27.
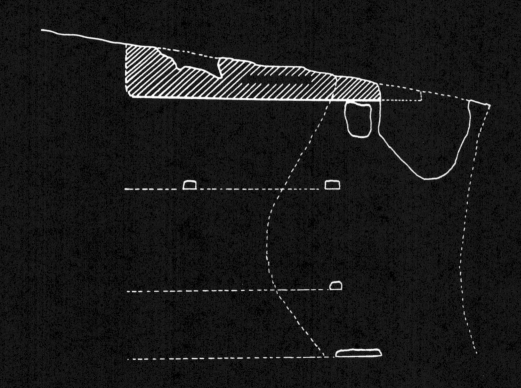

28.

The world news was as bad as it gets: Germany had invaded Poland and the short-term outlook was a bomb waiting to go off. The market for strategic metals [was on an upward trend and] the price of mercury [rose] significantly. The war in Europe spread. There was a shortage of spare parts, tires and so on. But Nuevo Mercurio was important for the Allies, so diesel continued to be supplied [from] the United States in tank trucks or drums loaded [onto] pickups.

29.

Mercury was one of the seven original metals designated as strategic, and the search for these minerals was begun on July 1, 1939, and extended throughout World War II.
  The disruption of ocean transportation and close relationship of Italy and Spain to the Axis powers made it necessary for the United States to develop alternative sources of mercury. Mexico, for years the second largest mercury producer in the area, appeared to be the most promising source of appreciable quantities. In...1941, an agreement was reached for the United States to obtain surplus production of mercury placed under export control by the Mexican Government.
  Virtually all of Mexico's mercury output [was] exported. The United States received most of the Mexican metal.

30.

Nuevo Mercurio [grew] rapidly. Wooden houses [were] replaced by adobe dwellings; clothes shops and grocery stores appeared. The primary school [was] completed and functioning. And a [new] branch of the National Union of Mine and Metallurgic Workers of the Mexican Republic was opened....They had been told that the statutes for implementation would be sent from Mexico City.

31.

The Company had its own doctor....He'd come from Nueva Rosita and was called Juan Palomares. The hospital...had x-ray equipment as the miners had to receive chest examinations every six months. Palomares took [the] first x-rays of the newly arrived and regular miners. These examinations were classified by the degree of silicosis [produced by inhalation of silica particles] they already suffered or had acquired. [But what] Palomares reported to the superintendent's office was [the] percentage of anthracosis [chronic inflammation of the bronchial tubes and lungs due to inhalation of dust containing carbon crystals], a condition only suffered by coal miners.

32.

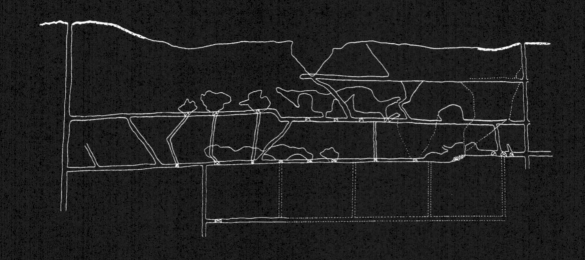

33.

A third level was opened up from the Veta Rica mineshaft. The
shaft was now deep enough to justify the installation of a loading
pocket....The Company [acquired] another furnace with a capacity
of 100 tons and [constructed] four vertical, iron-clad brick
smelters of the Scott design...20 tons per hour. They began to
sink a shaft adjacent to San Isidro in preparation for mining
[in conjunction with] the Glory Hole system. The slag heaps grew
larger [in] the landscape, altering [the] physiognomy of the site.

34.

I do believe this is Nuevo Mercurio. See, here it says Mine Workers Union. And it says something else too: something fraction something. The rest is unreadable. And then here, there's a baseball team, all turned out in smart kit, with their mitts and everything. It says Hotel Casino there, and there's the Casino beside it. I guess the building you can see here is the union office, there was an arcade [in front of] the entrance. [This looks like] the assembly room. Over there is an old fashioned cavalry uniform, with the breeches, the Federica boot, and the kepi. You can only see the necktie in profile, but it's the same boot and breeches. The military were there. I think they guarded the mercury en route to its destination. Because, in those days, it was a matter of national security. That much can be read. I'm pretty sure it is Nuevo Mercurio. What about you, what can you see?

Yes, the ecosystem is right. And the type of buildings; they are the same as now, or at least the few still standing. Look at the people in their hats, and the ladies. [That's] the main street, with the adobe houses and temporary roofs. Victoria, it says, that sounds like the name of the team. There's a man with a pith helmet, you can tell how old he is, he's got someone holding each arm. They're all well-dressed.

35.

In late 1944...the price of mercury plummeted. Mining was... suspended until the summer of 1947....The firm changed its trade name from Mercurios Mexicanos to the Compañía Minera Veta Rica, S.A.,...headed by Don Ignacio Martínez Flores, who put his nephew, Ignacio Martínez Flores, in charge. By that time, Glory Hole was in full production and the mine...at a good pace until 1962, when the price of mercury plummeted [again].

36.

A [jaw] crusher [was] installed in the San Isidro crib with
a steel coarse-ore bin and a belt-conveyor leading to a cone
crusher. The material then descended...to a brick-lined crusher,
with a capacity of 200 tons. At the back, an inclined belt
conveyor...fed the transporter belt, which in turn filled the
chutes of the furnaces.

37.
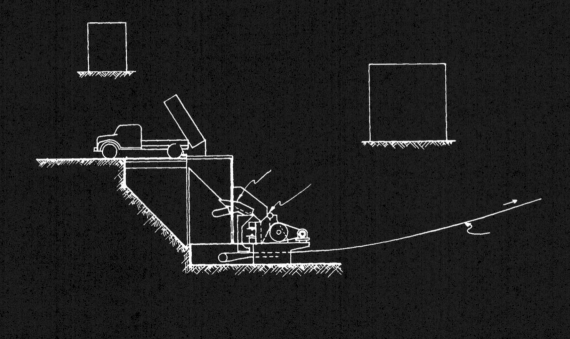

38.

Depending on the type of deposit, mercury ore is mined by either surface or underground methods. With either method, mercury mining is a comparatively small-scale operation because the deposits are characteristically small and irregular in size.

39.

Some miners [presented] with cases of hydrargyria,...mercury poisoning. The symptoms [are] trembling of the hands and mouth ulcers.

40.

It is essentially a distillation process in which mercury ore is heated in a mechanical furnace or retort to vaporize the mercury, followed by cooling and condensation of the vapor to liquid metal. Recovery of the mercury is high, averaging about 95 percent for furnace plants and 98 percent for retort installations.

41.

The mercury remains [bioavailable] in the environment. It causes
renal failure and madness when the poisoning is very severe.
There's a point when you get brain damage.

42.
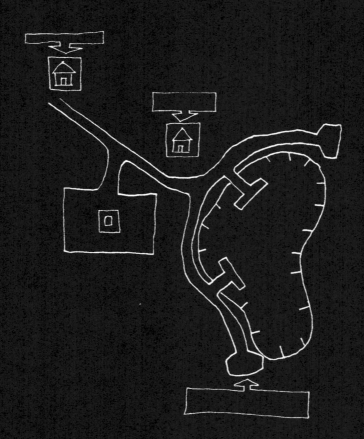

43.

In the beginning, they wouldn't let me down the mine because I was too young: just seventeen. [First], we constructed the Yankees' houses. The men formed a union. Later some people began to get political and that was the end of that. Then we formed [another]. It was the last one because the mining industry didn't want us there. After that, we joined the Confederation of Mexican Workers, with Fidel Velázquez. We were the last miners to have a union. [We used to have] a collective contract. I stopped working in the mine sometime in 73 or 74.

44.

Due to the expansion of mining activity, mainly associated with mercury extraction, the community reached a peak population of 10,000 inhabitants between 1940 and 1970. Unemployment-related migration began [in] 1975. [After that], the population shrank [by] 95%.

45.

Level 1 (A) - Extends 320 m to the east of Tiro General. A series of crosscuts were driven on either side to assess the limits and richness of the lode.

Level 2 (B) - Also extends 320 m to the east with a series of crosscuts on either side. To the east [there is also] a winze at 90 m...

Level 3 - extends 55 m to the east of shaft 30-6.

All these tunnels connect with Tiro General and Tiro San Isidro (except at level 3).

46.

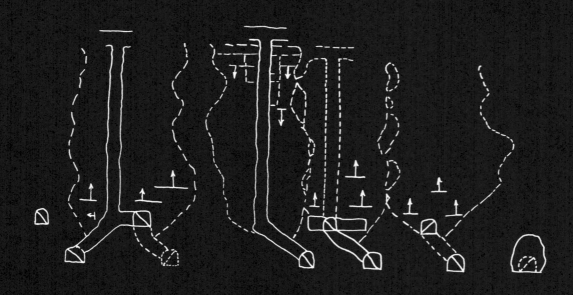

47.

The Company [was] unable to negotiate any contract that would allow it to sell its products at a profit. Moreover, the mineral lodes were not particularly rich: as the mines [became deeper], the cost of extraction [increased]....The Company [only] left a small group of watchmen, and the unionized miners [had to] present themselves before the arbitration committee in Fresnillo to receive their redundancy pay.

48.

In 1965, Ignacio Martínez sold the business to an engineer called Miguel Ángel Roca Cuellar, who again changed the trading name, this time to Mercurio Mexicano, S.A. de C.V. In 1970, a new Tiro General shaft was sunk, and, towards the end of the year, construction began on a flotation plant with a capacity of 400 tons per day. In 1972, a small access ramp was added to an old cut and ran from there to the edge of Glory Hole.
    Finally, on June..., all work was halted until, under the auspices of the Mining Commission, it was restarted on... June 29, 1974.

49.

[Mercury] was the key to everything here. And ["Long Tall"] José Espinosa knew that well. True enough, none of us leave this world without paying our debts. Seems he was just a poor peasant from the local area. But he got so much money that he made a clown of himself. I never saw it 'cos it was before my time, but a lot of people, my parents included, did. Seems like when he went to the toilet, he'd grab a...bill to [wipe himself]. When they used to send me for the rations, I'd have to take off my hat and act all respectful. But the minute he set eyes on so much money... well, you can imagine. An' I believe that was God's justice. Some of his nephews and nieces still live around here.

50.

Fall: 15th of December 1978.
  Early in the evening, a bolide visible over a radius of at least 200 km exploded with thunderous detonations over north-central Mexico, scattering meteorites over an elliptical area more than 10 km in length just north of the village of Nuevo Mercurio. Over 300 specimens were found, most with at least a partially retained fusion crust. The largest mass in early reports was 1.4 kg, but most stones were very small. The meteorite itself is a largely equilibrated H5 chondrite with olivine (Fa17.3) and pyroxene (Fs15.8) values within the normal H chondrite range.

51.

The mine finally closed down due to complaints from the health sector....One day, just like in a...movie, the people from the town began to suffer migraines. Adults and children. And as well as the headaches, they got nosebleeds. That was in the eighties.

52.

53.

I was working on a ranch called Santa Cruz, we'd finished for the
day and I was cycling home....It was like a huge ball of firewood
burning up there. That's right, in the sky. It was still early.
And then it went and exploded. You could hear it. And after
that there were lights, all around....They were all here by the
next day. Scientists from god only knows where. Said they'd been
following it. According to their calculations, they thought it'd
fall nearer Saltillo. The ones from Houston already knew. They
were full of explanations, and it seems this is the sort of place
where meteorites often fall. I hadn't heard that before. We'd
never seen anything like it. There are sometimes comet showers.
But they fall down an' break up, or that's what I think. They
tried to stop us taking anything at first. Nothing until they'd
finished studying it all. They said it might have radiation.
People turn up to look around now and again. But nobody's been
for a while now.

54.

A rumor went around that nuclear waste had been dumped in Nuevo Mercurio. And at the same time a doctor who used to work with us—he's passed on now—told us that his...students [in] social services came to the region with the story that spontaneous miscarriages were a common occurrence and people often suffered nosebleeds. Those can all be symptoms of high blood pressure, but they weren't.

55.

During the inspection carried out by the Undersecretariat for Environmental Management of the Ministry for Health and Social Services, act No. 3548, dated July 5, 1980, in the installations of the ground surrounding Minera Rosicler, S.A., deposits of the following substances were identified: diesel, chlorine, polychlorinated biphenyls (PCBs) (42 200-litre drums), vinegar (6 200-litre drums), mining waste, catalytic mercury ash, solid waste (300-400 tons), corrosive substances (12 200-litre drums), solid and liquid waste (569 200-litre drums), and PCB ash to the west.

56.

The report also shows that the drums [containing polychlorinated biphenyls (PCBs) and other substances] had labels [identifying] their contents. At the time of the inspection, no mercury had been extracted by the company for a number of months and there were even signs of the mine being dismantled.

57.

All Latin American governments, irrespective of their political-ideological orientation, have encouraged the expansion of extractive activity as a measure for stimulating economic growth and sustaining public finances.

58.

Polychlorinated biphenyls (PCBs) are chlorinated hydrocarbons with the generic formula: $C_{12}H_{10-n}Cl_n$. [They are found in a variety of forms, ranging from oily liquids to waxy solids.]

59.

A complaint was filed against Clarence William Nugent and he was tried before the Attorney General's Office (PGR) in the Federal District of Mexico (Mexico City) by the then Special Clean-up Programs Office of the Undersecretariat for Environmental Management of the Ministry, as is shown in file 6/090 (724.1)/2, number ZP60054 of January 1981, accused of illegally importing these substances [from the United States], dumping the contents of an indeterminate number of drums into the abandoned mineshafts, ground spillages in the area around the mine, and smuggling.

60.

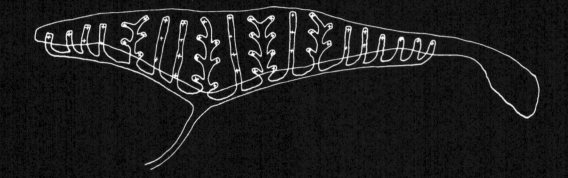

61.

We started to construct a town for them, a new Nuevo Mercurio. An alternative town. The houses [were made of] corrugated iron and earth....There's a potable water supply, over there you can see the assembly room for the communal land group. There's no trace of toxic materials here [because] we're 4 km from the old Nuevo Mercurio. But the people didn't want to leave their town. The majority stayed. The population varies...many people are returning due to Trump's repatriation program and sometimes the children [who come back] don't speak Spanish. [The situation is] complex: a teacher earns Mex$1,200 a month and a kilo of mercury brings in Mex$2,400.

62.

The PCBs were produced by the transnational company Monsanto and the other dangerous waste by Diamond Shamrock (an oil company), Monochem (now called Borden; industrial chemicals and synthetics), BF Goodrich (tires), PPG Industries (...paints and coatings).

63.

We weren't allowed to go there. They were afraid that there might be radioactivity. They said, "You'll die, you'll get cancer."... Complaints were made but all that happened was that the gringos left, the mine closed and no one had any work.

64.

On March 18, 1983, Clarence Nugent was found not guilty as there was no environmental jurisdiction related to the case.

65.

When [PCBs] are released, they have immediate or delayed detrimental effects on the environment due to bioaccumulation and/or toxic effects on the biotic system. PCBs with high chlorination levels can cause disorders in the reproductive apparatuses of living beings and impede development and growth in plants. Some [animal] studies have indicated problems with liver enlargement... due to the effort needed to eliminate the chemicals. More recent research...has concluded that PCBs are carcinogenic.

66.

It was an odyssey. There were no roads. When we got there, we saw a town that had been magnificent in its day. Buildings, a hospital with x-ray equipment. They even say that when extraction was at its peak, they brought the Dodgers in from Los Angeles to play against the miners....They also had light aircraft and a [landing strip].

67.

There were no indications of above-normal levels of radioactivity in the area visited.
   No radioactive material was found.
   In four locations, drums of polychlorinated biphenyls (PCBs) were found.

Recommendations:

1. Analyze the samples to identify the toxic substances present.
2. Undertake social, clinical, biological, and economic studies to determine the impact of these substances within a radius of 3 km as it has been found that families use drums that may have come from the mine for domestic purposes.
3. Mark out the perimeter of the mine and install warning signs.
4. Recover the drums and ash for secure storage.
5. Schedule another visit to inspect the interior of the mine.

68.

Since environmental laws were very lax....That's the way capitalism works: reduce costs and increase profits....PCBs were used as fuel for the retort furnaces. They were cheaper than diesel.

69.

It's a very poor, barren zone. When I went there, I thought I'd only ever seen those kinds of images on news programs about Biafran children.

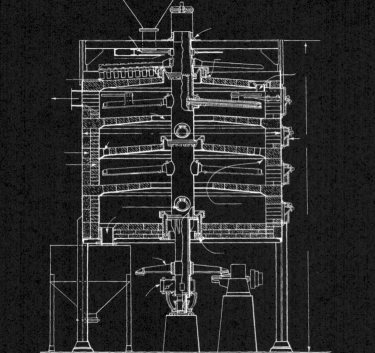

71.

The people in the community used some of the [PCB] drums to construct fences and/or roofs for their homes....According to the residents, the contents of the drums were burned in furnaces at about 800 m from their dwellings, within the precincts of the mine.

72.

Assistant machine operator, machine operator, shoveler for track clearing: I did it all....This was the last [mine] I worked in ....There were so many longstanding injustices. Governments were all different back then. They wanted to do things first one way and then another and another. No, I don't have no time for that.

73.

The substances came in large drums labelled "Alcohol de verduras" (vinegar). It's a mildly toxic waste product of leaching. Inside each drum was a smaller one labelled PCB. It was a serious smuggling operation. It's said that [the gringo] did this when the whole world signed an agreement to stop producing PCBs. In the United States they make a great fuss if a single drop of the stuff spills over. There has to be a clean-up operation. Nature is powerless against those substances; they are very stable, take a long time to break down. What's more, they are easily absorbed through the skin. The higher the level of fat in a body, the greater the quantity absorbed and so the poison acts more rapidly. The effects aren't hereditary....But things have a way of protecting themselves, right? Their bodies were so undernourished, they absorbed less of the substance.

74.

Life tries to find its own courses. Some species become resistant to pollutants and clean the ground. There are certain species in Zacatecas that have developed this phytomining ability.

75.

The process for breaking down PCBs requires a furnace capable of creating temperatures over 6000 degrees Celsius, hotter than the chromosphere of the sun.

76.

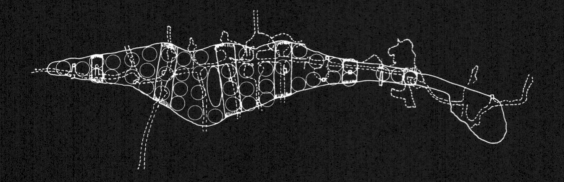

77.

Based on the preliminary study, we conclude that there is ground contamination of PCBs and mercury. The contamination is scattered around several locations in the community and, although the concentrations detected do not apparently exceed the regulations for PCB, these levels cannot be [considered] as definitive since the total concentration of PCB in the ground analyzed is not known.

78.

Mexico lacks the infrastructure to treat these substances...
they are exported to countries that have the relevant technical
capacity....There is evidence that, between 1995 and 1997, 2,903
tons of PBC left the country, with 1,406 tons going to Finland,
664 to Holland, 460 to the United States, 371 to England, and 2
to France.

79.

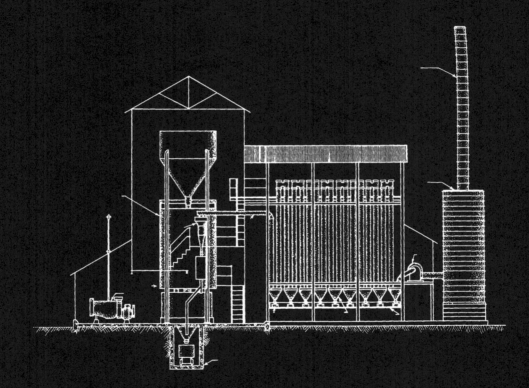

80.

When we spoke to the caretaker of the mine, he gave us his version. A gringo turned up and paid everyone to help him take the drums from the mine, [then] they piled them up and burned them for hours. The ash was like snow, a fine, pure white powder. They said that when it rained or was very windy, the powder used to get inside their houses and they started to have headaches and their blood pressure went up. That was when we began to understand what was going on.

81.

People jumped over the fence, they emptied the drums right
there and took them to collect water. There were traces of PCB
[remaining in the drums]. When we found out exactly what the stuff
was, we realized the danger. People were victims of their own
and that gringo's greed. Someone's responsible for all this. We
submitted a report on our findings to the SEDUVE [Ministry for
Urban and Ecological Development]. That report can't be found now.
Someone went and lost it.

82.

Whenever they fall, a lot of investigators turn up here the next day to collect them. There's no proof, but there is a rule: in certain circumstances, mercury produces a magnetic field....Even soldiers come to buy the stones.

83.

In November 2001, a delegation from the state branch of the SEMARNAT [Secretariat of Environment and Natural Resources] called a meeting. The Universidad Autónoma de Zacatecas was represented by the School of Mining, Metallurgy, and Geology and the Faculty of Chemical Sciences; also represented were: the Federal Attorney's Office for Environmental Protection; the State Government Secretariat for Public Works; the Municipal President's Office of Mazapil, and the Community of San Felipe Nuevo Mercurio. It was decided to undertake...actions to contain the contamination, which were completed in March 2002.

84.

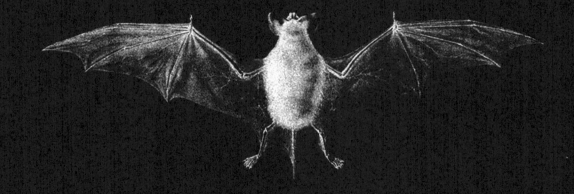

85.

I have an uncle, Mom's brother, who's a metallurgic engineer. [He] worked there. He's in a gold mine in the Durango Sierra now. I don't know, strange things happen. They said that there were elves in the [Nuevo Mercurio] mines. Tiny green elves. A couple of times, I got the courage to ask my uncle about them and he was frightened. I don't remember, he said. But what were they like? I asked. They were this small and green. I think the poison had already got to them and they were seeing things.

86.

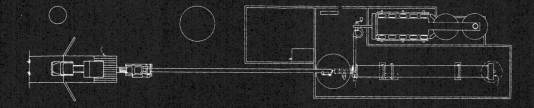

87.

Lowering the drums down the mineshaft was a bad idea. The freshwater table passes through there. Drums don't last forever, they corrode and the PCB seeps out....They say there are still around three thousand in the shaft, and that some of them have tipped over, and the contents are leaking....It was the owner who ordered them to be put down there. A grille was installed, and then he had the winch removed so we couldn't go down there. The townsfolk were pleased because all that meant paid work. They killed a porker and a cow to celebrate. But they left a long-term problem there. And let's hope we don't live to see its results.

88.

There's a colony of *Tadarida brasiliensis*....Bats....They produce tons of guano, a high-quality fertilizer. It sells at Mex$15,000 a ton. I've never been able to see them because I have a pacemaker and you have to descend about 80 meters.

89.

The remedy was limited to confinement, putting up signs. They buried everything. The Mexican way of doing things.

90.

The inhabitants still extract metallic mercury in homemade furnaces and the communal artisanal furnaces found in mining regions. The level of mercury contamination in the area of study is critical. Despite the fact that extraction no longer takes place on an industrial scale, there is still contamination.

91.

The catchword for this phenomenon is "neo-extractivism," where "neo" signals a certain degree of continuity with historical trends that began with the conquest and colonization of Latin America and Africa 500 years ago....The scale and rhythm of extractive activities have reached unprecedented levels since the turn of the [21st] century, as capital scours the planet in search of speculative and productive investments in the context of overlapping crises: economic, financial, food, environmental.

92.

Development...Ecotourism Project, "Bats of San Felipe Nuevo Mercurio."

The abandoned mine works of Nuevo Mercurio have been colonized by between eighty and ninety thousand bats of the species *Tadarida brasiliensis* and *Plecotus mexicanus*. Both insectivore species are of great environmental importance due to their role in pest control. It is at present the largest Chiroptera colony in Zacatecas State.

- Clean the site of the former Mina de Fomenta Minero and construct a visitor center
- Construct walkways and observation platforms around the bats' habitat.
- Build a fence to ensure visitor safety.
- [Place] explanatory signage related to the site and its fauna ...and further signs on the highway [to] offer information.
- Print information booklets.
- [Offer] ecotourism training courses for interested townspeople.

93.

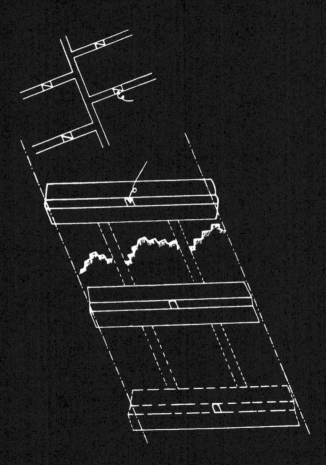

94.

Well, there's always been some production. There are still a few people working, though not many at all. But they do extract stuff. Now, why would I lie to you? You can hear the echo of all that movement in the past....No, no, the bats only arrived a short a while back.

95.

It's not easy to accurately assess the total non-carcinogenic risk to the population as we have not yet established the total exposure (to date, 209 related items have been identified but only 14 have so far been analyzed in this part of the study). However, it is clear that the community suffers from chronic exposure, and PCBs are capable of causing neuro-behavioral disorders and damage to the endocrine system at low concentrations with prolonged exposure.

96.

We're out, we're all out now. Done for the day.
How much have you got? Ten kilos?
Naaah.
You haven't got much, have you?
Yeah, haven't got much today. We're going deep down. It doesn't want to be found.
Why?
The rock's so hard now.
Ahhh.
Yes, it's real hard that deep down.
Come on, cheer up.
Haven't you even filled one of those little white containers?
I've got two.
Two? Not much. Are two of those half a large one?
That's right. It's a half. The problem is all the dust.
These people are lazy. The ones who work over there just keep going and they get more out.

97.

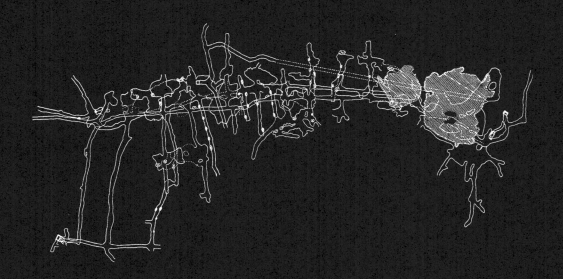

98.

Is sustainable capitalism really possible? According to O'Connor, who poses the question in what has now become a classic text for ecosocialists, the short answer is "no" and the longer answer is "probably not."

99.

Rare-earth elements [induce] luminescence when doped in calcium.
   In the Mexican chrondite Nuevo Mercurio (c) [the meteorite that fell in 1975], Raman spectroscopy has detected phases of [luminescent] calcium phosphate, anhydrous merrillite, and such hydrates as chloroapatite and hydroxiapatite....The specific extra-terrestrial origin of the calcium phosphates offers foreign chemical impurities...in the presence of $CaPO_4$ structures....The study...enabled...to clearly identify the merrillite and apatites and to confirm the differences between the terrestrial and extra-terrestrial $CaPO_4$.

100.

The tunnels run almost as far as where we were in the Rosicler [mine]. Think of it, down below, there's just the one entrance but there are a lot of [tunnels] and a whole load of ways out. If you don't know where you're going, it's easy to get lost.

## List of Sources

## a.

**Text:**
Rewriting of the short story "El huésped" by Amparo Dávila, originally published in 1959. The rewriting mainly consists of: substituting the characters "the houseguest" and "Guadalupe" for "The Company" and "the machine," respectively; transposing the verb tenses into the future, using "will" where appropriate and the narrative voice to the second person singular. [CMacS: Although there is an existing translation of the story by Audrey Harris and Matthew Gleeson in *The Houseguest: And Other Stories* (W.W. Norton & Co, 2018), I have decided to retranslate the text to accommodate the above changes.]

**Graphic Elements:**
Fragments of pictograms generated by Mayer Sasson's program for Manuel Felguérez's 1975 *La máquina estética* (*The Aesthetic Machine*).

**Studio Photographs:**
Taken by Elizabeth del Ángel, stones found in the Nuevo Mercurio mines, pp. 12, 15, 35, 39, 46, 50, 62, 67, 73, 82, and 83.

**Archive Photographs:**
Drums of polychlorinated biphenyl and ash in Nuevo Mercurio, taken in 1986 by Dr. Héctor René Vega Carrillo, pp. 17, 44, and 84

**High-contrast Photographs:**
Taken by Verónica Gerber Bicecci during a journey to do fieldwork in San Felipe Nuevo Mercurio.

# b.

**Text:**
1., 4., 5., 8., 10., 12., 17., 21., 23., 25., 28., 30., 31., 33., 36., 39., 47., and 49. From "José Largo" ("Long Tall José"), a story written by José Luis Martínez P. The text is dedicated to his daughter Blanca Inés, who created a handmade edition in honor of her father.

41., 54., 66., 69., 73., 74., 75., 80., 81., and 87. Conversation with Dr. Hugo Vega Carrillo in his cubicle at the Unidad Académica de Estudios Nucleares of the Universidad Autónoma de Zacatecas, August 2018.

44., 45., 55., 56., 64., 71., 77., 90., and 95. From *Evaluación de riesgo en dos sitios contaminados por bifenilos policlorados (BPC) y metales pesados*, PhD dissertation in Environmental Sciences, submitted by Rogelio Costilla Salazar (M.Sc.), Universidad Autónoma de San Luis Potosí, Faculties of Chemical Sciences, Engineering and Medicine, multidisciplinary course of the Environmental Sciences Postgraduate Degree Program, May 2010.

2., 3., 16., 18., and 26. From section "Región minera de Nuevo Mercurio" in *Diagnóstico integral sobre minería del estado de Zacatecas*, undated.

9., 15., 29., 38., and 40. From *Mercury. A Materials Survey*, by James W. Pennington, United States Printing Office, Department of Interior, Bureau of Mines, Washington, 1959.

22., 43., 53., 72., and 94. Conversation with the miner José Esquivel outside the Tiro General mine, August 2018.

51., 63., 68., 85., and 89. Conversation with the journalist Alfredo Valadez Rodríguez in La Cofradía restaurant, August 2018.

14., 20., 35., and 48. From *1. Estudio geológico minero de la zona de brecha San Isidro en Nuevo Mercurio, Zacatecas, y proposición de un método para su explotación and 2. Tratamientos piro e hidrometalúrgicos del cinabrio y perspectivas futuras para el beneficio económico del mismo*, thesis for the professional title of Mining and Metallurgic Engineer, submitted by José Juan Gurrola Vargas, Universidad Autónoma de Zacatecas, School of Mining and Metallurgy, 1975.

58., 65., and 78. From a letter to delegates and senators "Con punto de acuerdo, por el que se propone que la Secretaría de Medio Ambiente y Recursos Naturales ordene que se lleven a cabo la sustitución, el manejo y la disposición final de los bifenilos policlorados, así como equipos y materiales que los contienen, donde quiera que estos se ubiquen, presentada por el diputado Fernando Espino Arévalo, del grupo parlamentario del PVEM," handed in at the Palacio Legislativo, San Lázaro, headquarters of the Cámara de Diputados del Honorable Congreso de la Unión de los Estados Unidos Mexicanos, D.F., on March 30, 2004.

57., 91., and 98. From "Capitalism Versus the Environment" by Darcy Tetreault, in *The Essential Guide to Critical Development Studies*, Henry Veltmeyer and Paul Bowles (Eds): Routledge, 2017.

61., 82., and 88. Conversation with Dr. Manuel Macías Patiño during our journey to San Felipe Nuevo Mercurio, August 2018.

59. and 83. From the report "Contención de residuos de bifenilos policlorados en la comunidad de San Felipe Nuevo Mercurio, Mazapil, Zacatecas. Una experiencia en el estado," SEMARNAT, INE and Gobierno del Estado de Zacatecas, April 2002.

6. Conversation in the home of Dr. Bernardo del Hoyo, August 2018.

34. Conversation between Dr. Manuel Macías Patiño and Dr. Miguel Ángel Díaz Castorena while looking at an old photograph from the archive of the Delgadillo family, who act as caretakers of the Rosicler mine and surrounding areas, August 2018.

50. From "Nuevo Mercurio meteorite," available at: https://www.mindat.org/loc-266007.html. Accessed: June 17, 2019.

62. From "Mina zacatecana convertida en un cementerio tóxico" by Alfredo Valadez Rodríguez, in *La Jornada*, "Estados," Monday August 23, 2010.

67. From "Reporte de la inspección de la mina Rosicler de la comunidad de Nuevo Mercurio CREN/RI-NVOHG-1/310186," undertaken by Dr. Hugo René Vega Carrillo and the team of the Centro Regional de Estudios Nucleares, Universidad Autónoma de Zacatecas, January 1986.

71. From the final report "Generar Información Cualitativa y Cuantitativa de las Fuentes Minero-Metalúrgicas en México, Contrato No. INECC/RPA1-001/201,7" prepared by Martínez Arroyo A., Páramo Figueroa V. H., Gavilán García A., Martínez Cordero M. A., and Ramírez Muñoz T. for the Coordinación General de Contaminación y Salud Ambiental of the Instituto Nacional de Ecología y Cambio Climático, 2017.

92. From the PowerPoint "Plan de confinamiento de la mina del fomento minero San Felipe, Nuevo Mercurio" by Winni Schmidt, Institutional development project for management of contaminated sites, Dirección General de Investigación sobre la Contaminación Urbana y Regional, Investigación sobre Sustancias Químicas y Riesgos Ecotoxicológicos, SEMARNAT, GTZ, Zacatecas, 2002.

96. Conversation between prospectors and Sr. Delgadillo at the mine head, August 2018.

99. From *Estudio de meteoritos singulares por técnicas espectroscópicas y de luminiscencia no destructivas*, PhD thesis in Chemical Sciences, submitted by Laura Tormo Cifuentes, Universidad Autónoma de Madrid, Facultad de Ciencias, Departamento de Geología y Geoquímica y Consejo Superior de Investigaciones Científicas, 2013.

100. Conversation with Sr. Delgadillo, the current caretaker of the mine, August 2018.

```
Diagrams:
```
19. Geological section at co-ordinate 3200 N; 27. Section 15–15 first cut without ramp; 46. Sections A–A and B–B; 60. Haulage level seen from above; 76. Aerial view of level 4 or B; 93. Sketch showing a level mined with descending cuts, taken from *1. Estudio geológico minero de la zona de brecha San Isidro en Nuevo Mercurio Zacatecas . . . .* op. cit.

32. Aerial view, longitudinal section; 97. Development of level 3 of the Tiro General mine, taken from *Exploración y desarrollo del nivel 3° (C) de la mina Tiro General de la Unidad Nuevo Mercurio de la C.F.M. Estudio económico comparativo en los procesos pirometalúrgicos de mineral y concentrado de mercurio.* Thesis for the professional title of Mining and Metallurgical Engineer, submitted by Rafael Reyes Macías, Universidad Autónoma de Zacatecas, Escuela de Minas y Metalurgia, 1980.

7. Reinterpretation of the map of historical meteorite craters in Zacatecas State by Dr. Bernardo del Hoyo.

11. Map of the route from Zacatecas to Nuevo Mercurio, taken from "Reporte de la inspección de la mina Rosicler de la comunidad de Nuevo Mercurio CREN/RI-NVOHG-1/310186," op. cit.

13. Section Through D Retort; 24. Section Through Rotary Furnace; 37. Layout–Rotary Furnace Plant (fragment); 70. Section Through Multiple-Hearth Furnace; 79. Layout—Multiple-Hearth Furnace Plant; 86. Layout—Rotary Furnace Plant, taken from *Mercury. A Materials Survey*, op. cit.

42. (Redrawn) plan of the walkways and platforms for the ecotourism project Murciélagos de San Felipe, Nuevo Mercurio, taken from "Plan de confinamiento de la mina del fomento minero San Felipe, Nuevo Mercurio," op cit.

52. *Plecotus auritus*, detail from illustration 67, in *Kunstformen der Natur* (1904), by Ernst Haeckel, taken from Wikimedia Commons.

84. *Nyctinomus brasiliensis* (new Latin name: *Tadarida brasiliensis*), in *Iconographia Zoologica* (1881-1883), taken from Wikimedia Commons.

# Epilogue

Barefoot in the field,
I will feel the creditor-earth
on my naked soles

Cristina Rivera Garza[1]

[1] A shorter version of this text accompanied Verónica Gerber Bicecci's exhibition *Barefoot feet, the fields in them, I will feel the creditor of the land on my bare soles*, Proyectos Monclova, Mexico City, Jan. 23 - March 3. Tr. Christopher Fraga.

## The Beginning of Extraction

Mercury is a rocky planet and a Roman God. Astrology has endowed it with the ability to transmit messages speedily or, when weak, to complicate understanding and travel. Mercury, also known as quicksilver due to its bright, silvery-white color and density, is a chemical element and transition metal found, in its free state, in small quantities in the Earth's core, but it is plentiful in cinnabar, a bright red mineral composed of 85% mercury and 15% sulfur: mercury sulfide. It was in that vermillion form that a certain Long Tall José found it on one side of the Cerro del Calvo, while following bees in search of honey. Shortly afterward—sometime around November 1935—Eusebio Gaucín, recently arrived from Fresnillo, told him that he was searching for mercury on his boss's orders, and when Long Tall José heard the description of the reddish rock, he took out a couple of samples from his ixtle sack. According to the legend of the founding of San Felipe Nuevo Mercurio,

that conversation led to the beginning of the
most constant and profitable mercury extraction
project in 20th-century Mexico.

**Disappropriation**
We learn all this—or rather, gather it—from the
series of textual juxtapositions that make up
part b. of *La Compañía* (*The Company*), the mural-
book Verónica Gerber Bicecci exhibited in the
FEMSA biennial in 2018, published by Almadía in
2019. Far from facilitating the task by offering
a chronological or personal interpretation
of the events, Gerber Bicecci displays the
selected material, with its uneven borders and
particular languages. An original text, written
by José Luis Martínez P. and published in a
handmade edition by his daughter (to whom the
text is dedicated in the original version); a
series of conversations with academics from the
Unidad Académica de Estudios Nucleares of the
Universidad Autónoma de Zacatecas; an article
from the newspaper *La Jornada*; metallurgic

reports in English dating from the 1950s and others in Spanish produced twenty years later; a few undergraduate and doctoral theses; secondary sources such as "Capitalism Versus the Environment" by Darcy Tetreault, in *The Essential Guide to Critical Development Studies*; a conversation with a miner; a PowerPoint presentation of regional contamination, prepared by SEMARNAT. In the appendix of sources, it is possible to verify the textual or spoken origins of each of the selected sections included in the second part of *The Company*, where—from the outside, not within—the past, present, and even the future of a mining town on the Mexican Altiplano are reconfigured. This procedure, which escapes by a hair's breadth the bibliographic sections of academic works, nonetheless has the virtue of distancing the project from the appropriation strategies that have been rightly questioned by art and literary critics of the early twenty-first century, converting *The Company* into an exemplary disappropriative work.[2]

2. For a general discussion of disappropriation, see Cristina Rivera Garza, *The Restless Dead: Necrowriting and Disappropriation*. (Vanderbilt University Press, 2020. Tr. Robin Myers).

Nothing is hidden. Here—in contrast to the advice of the authors of Great Twentieth-Century Literature—everything is shown, seams and all. When passing from one page to the next, from one photo to another, it is clear that nothing we see is the result of mysterious, inexplicable, individual, authorial inspiration. Rather, it is the product of research and the selection of material from the world we share. All those materials are present, not so much for us to recognize as to recognize ourselves in them. Like any good disappropriationist, Gerber Bicecci repeatedly shows that a work is an appointment we—readers, material, and author—turn up to, if we wish, at the same time. Here, we have stopped to look, to see, in the materiality of the book or the exhibition, in order to resolve and compare, interpret and define, as we come to articulate and know ourselves. This is a conversation, a happening whose script is scarcely sketched out by a set of decisions for which, nevertheless, the author remains fully responsible: the choice and placement of the materials. From then on, the experience is ours. From then on, the responsibility and its implications rest on us. Never before has it been possible to say, in the strictest sense, that the author is the reader—and vice versa—as in this type of disappropriative work.

**Materialization and Ethics**
The opposite of the imperialist concept of giving voice is showcasing a series of voices that already exist. And, in addition, producing the listening operation that allows these real, concrete voices to reach the ears of others. To achieve this, we do not need the words of the author (and what, in a world like ours, would the words of an author be?), but the words of those practitioners of a common language in which, as writers, we participate and from which, at the given moment, we borrow. The palpable recognition of those loans, which lead to a debt that cannot be guaranteed or repaid by any form of credit, is the ethical foundation of the

project of radical materialization in the most recent work of Verónica Gerber Bicecci.[3] To access that work, we have to distance ourselves from the illusion of origin and accept that everything has a pre-existence and that nothing has ever been said for the first or only time. In the words of José Revueltas, we have to accept that we follow in the footsteps of others.[4] Those marks on the surface of the Earth, denoting the absence of others, are part of the first great questions about bodies: Why are they no longer here? Why are we in their place? Whose place do I occupy here? With whom do I share my existence at this point in the universe? Addressing those questions leads to concepts of territory, and of writing, which include the sediments of the soil and the air, and the human and non-human presence among them.

**The Surpassing Disaster and Re-writing**
In the first part of *The Company*, Verónica Gerber Bicecci sets out to rewrite what is now

[3]. For the concept of an unpayable debt, see Fred Moten and Stefano Harvey, *The Undercommons: Fugitive Planning & Black Study* (Minor Compositions, 2003).

[4]. José Revueltas, "El escritor y la tierra" in *Visión del Paricutín, José Revueltas. 6. Obra Reunida. Crónica* (Era, 2014).

a classic text of Mexican literature. Amparo
Dávila, the Zacatecas author associated with
the Generación de Medio Siglo (the Mid-century
Generation) published her best known text, "El
huésped" (The Houseguest), in 1959 as part of her
book *Tiempo destrozado* (*Destroyed Time*). By then,
mercury mining was well established in San Felipe
Nuevo Mercurio, but nothing had changed for the
better and much had worsened in the dry, desolate
geography of the mining zones of Zacatecas State.
Verónica Gerber Bicecci rewrites the story word-
for-word, intervening only to make a few subtle
but significant changes in the text: rather than
a first-person narrative, the story is now told
in the second person, with its imperative tone;
and instead of being set in the present, the
majority of the verbs are written in the simple
future tense with "will," from which nobody
escapes. In addition, the ominous, unnamable
presence of the original story now becomes
The Company of the title, while Guadalupe,
the domestic helper with whom the narrator

establishes an uneasy relationship of complicity in opposition to the undesired guest, is now the machine. These minor interventions, taken in combination with the photographs, which in turn are intervened by the superimposition of images by Manuel Felguérez (another Zacatecas artist), form a series of layers of meaning and experience that not only record the passage of time, but also what Jalal Toufic calls the "surpassing disaster."

   The fact is that the mass extraction of mercury in the Zacatecas mines—particularly during the period of the Second World War, when all Mexican production from the Altiplano was exported to the United States—has contaminated the ground and has had lasting effects on the bodies and minds of the residents of San Felipe Nuevo Mercurio and its surroundings. The pitted earth and cases of cancer or mental illness testify to the disaster that the capitalist extraction of quicksilver has brought about in the region. What makes the disaster surpassing, however, is the immaterial withdrawal of tradition. To quote Toufic, the "immaterial withdrawal of literary, philosophical, and thoughtful texts as well as of certain films, videos, and musical works, notwithstanding that copies of these continue to be physically available; of paintings and buildings that were not physically destroyed; of spiritual guides; and of the holiness/ specialness of certain spaces. In other words, whether a disaster is a surpassing one (for a community—defined by its sensibility to the immaterial withdrawal that results from such a disaster) cannot be ascertained by the number of casualties, the intensity of psychic traumas and the extent of material damage, but by whether we encounter in its aftermath symptoms of withdrawal of tradition."[5] Like the proverbial vampire before the mirror, tradition and its practices are there, or here, but inaccessible to sight or experience. To recover that access to withdrawn tradition, it is necessary to raise it as an issue, that is to say, make it part of present

5. Jalal Toufic, "The Withdrawal of Tradition Past a Surpassing Disaster," in Walid Raad, *Scratching on Things I Would Disavow: A History of Modern and Contemporary Art in the Arab World*, Part I, Volume I, Chapter I (Beirut: 1992–2005), ed. Clara Kim (Los Angeles: California Institute of the Arts/redcat, 2009).

dialogues and processes. Thus, what Toufic terms "resurrection" and I call "disappropriation" inevitably passes through re-writing.

Re-writing a text is never an innocent practice. It is, in the first instance, the process of selection, which often includes an exhaustive revision of the contexts of the production and distribution of works that come to us from the past. And after that come the real mechanisms of intervention that, by updating the works, include them in the concrete dialogues of the present. The words may be exactly the same as in the original text, or vary subtly, as in this case, but the work involved in preparing a text for a meeting with the here and now is undoubtedly comparable to the resurrection Toufic talks about. Those who re-write unleash the tradition that the surpassing disaster has rendered invisible or mute. Those who rewrite remove chains. Unhitch. They call up not so much the ghosts of the past as the continuities that, from the past, forge a practice of resistance to and contempt for the present. And that is why the emphasis Gerber Bicecci places on the violent and self-protective activity of The Company, as the indecipherable but perennial presence that holds terrified women in a house, brings to light the critique of gender and the combined threat of heteropatriarchy and capital that many of Dávila's readers downplayed or simply ignored throughout the twentieth century. So Gerber Bicecci returns to the archive of culture— stories, painting, theses, scientific reports, and technology—less to confirm or uncover it, as to activate it. What we are presented with is not ruins—if by that we understand, as Gordillo suggests, "dead things from a dead past"— but rubble. Rubble is still more distant from form and intrinsic to all habitable terrain, and results from the destruction of space, but without falling under the homogenizing spell of the past or the fetishizing effect of the present.[6] The future-tense conjugation of verbs in the first part of *The Company* is an indication

6. For an analysis of rubble vs. ruin, see Gustavo Gordillo, *Rubble: The Afterlife of Destruction* (Duke University Press, 2014).

that the activation of the archive not only moves back toward the past but also reaches forward to speculation about the future, where the threat of climate disaster and terricide looms as a probability rather than a possibility.[7]

## Translation as Algorithm as Translation

If we are to believe the projections of *La máquina distópica*[8] (*The Dystopian Machine*)—the web-based oracle resulting from the collaboration of Verónica Gerber Bicecci, Canek Zapata, and Carlos Bergen—in the year 2176, with 84% contamination and a 1-to-1 replacement of human labor, the future holds the following for us: "Barefoot in the field, I will feel the creditor-earth on my naked soles." Here again the words of Amparo Dávila, now generated by a text bot, and the images of Manuel Felguérez's *La máquina estética* (*The Aesthetic Machine*) do what had already been done in the past, which was to generate new geometric arrangements as the instructions changed, like the microscopic samples of polluted

[7] The concept of terricide is taken from Stuart Elden, "Terricide" in *Progressive Geographies*, (May 1, 2013). Available at: https://progressivegeographies.com/2013/02/08/terricide-lefebvre-geopolitics-and-the-killing-of-the-earth/

[8] This piece was developed in parallel with *La Compañía* and can be seen on: www.lamaquinadistopica.xyz (editors' note).

water from the El Bote mine, also in Zacatecas. Here, technology and collective work confront us with the future, but science fiction has now— in the blink of an eye, with the rapid change of instructions—become another form of natural history. The speculation that results from "what if?" propels us to unimagined points in time, while also taking us backward, in spatial terms, to the microscopic figure of inorganic life living in the water. From the stratum of the planets to the infinitesimal existence of the microbe or bacterium, passing through the scale of the human body, Gerber Bicecci's work does not allow us to forget the present, the moment when the oracle's messages are generated, and ultimately revealed danger. Here we are. This is what we share. This is our abyss. And, in this way, the visual artist who writes also becomes an activist.

Beyond developing a narrative arc of extractivism, the Anthropocene, or ecofeminism, obliging us to reach some crisis or learn some lesson, *La máquina distópica* offers a different arrangement, another version of the elements that have been laid out in *The Company*. Thanks to the algorithm, what happens is a translation in the widest sense of the term. The team behind *La máquina distópica* moves not only the position of the signified, reconfiguring it in each experiment, but also of the signifier, including the semiotic or a-signifying elements that escape, or attempt to escape, any form of subjective capture. A translation made under the auspices of radical materialism cannot do otherwise. And that is perhaps exactly the project underlying the greater part of Gerber's machine in our day: crossing the boundaries between disciplines and genres, between signifying and a-signifying material, through operations of translation that include a variety of technologies, fetching and carrying personal and other's materials, questioning them along the way, thereby achieving critical contact with them.

## Toward a Geology of Zacatecas

In "Las edades del cadáver" (The Ages of the Corpse), Sergio Villalobos-Ruminott argues that sovereignty and accumulation write upon the earth, albeit heterographically rather than directly.[9] This involves a "secret tattooing" that leaves a trace "of the material impact of bodies in their distribution across a territory." There is thus no way to decipher such a tattoo, which we all share and which marks us equally, without unearthing the processes by which capital and its allies, the hetero-patriarchy and racism, accumulate. If we are interested in the question of justice, we must dig into the layers of material that make up the supposed immutability of our world, de-sedimenting the origin myths and the languages of violence with which they have been articulated. With her physical presence in the mines and mining towns, her conversations with former miners and scientists, her readings of every variety of local documentation and of transnational edicts, Gerber Bicecci again and

9. Sergio Villalobos-Ruminott, "Las edades del cadáver: dictadura, guerra, desaparición (Postulados para una geología general)" in *Historiografía de la violencia. Historia, nihilismo, destrucción* (Ediciones La Cebra, 2016).

again raises—in every possible translation, including that exercised here by the passage of time and the attraction of space—the question of accumulation. And the result is not only a collective deciphering of that secret tattoo with which exploitation and despoliation have marked us, but something more. Activated by our reading, Gerber Bicecci moves us toward the past and the future, without for an instant forgetting the present we share, and restores our face and our body, along with the faces and bodies of others, multiplied as potency. Nothing is at peace here, everything is at stake.

**Verónica Gerber Bicecci** is a visual artist who writes. Her works include the series of drawings *Diagrams of Silence*, an exercise in visual exhumation based on the punctuation of various poems, and *Mudanza* (2010), a collection of essays about writers who deserted conventional literature to become visual artists. She currently coordinates, with Guillermo Espinosa Estrada, the Permanent Diagonal Writing Workshop in Mexico City. More at: www.veronicagerberbicecci.net

**Christina MacSweeney** is the translator of Valeria Luiselli's *The Story of My Teeth*, which received the 2016 Valle Inclán Translation Prize and was also shortlisted for the Dublin Literary Award. Her translations include collaborations with Daniel Saldaña París, Elvira Navarro, Julián Herbert, Jazmina Barrera, and Karla Suárez.

**Cristina Rivera Garza** is the acclaimed author of *The Iliac Crest*, *The Taiga Syndrome*, *Liliana's Invincible Summer*, and *Ningún reloj cuenta esto*, among other books. She is the recipient of a MacArthur Fellowship, the Sor Juana Inés de la Cruz Prize, and the Anna Seghers Prize. Rivera Garza was awarded the 2024 Pulitzer Prize in Memoir for *Liliana's Invincible Summer: A Sister's Search for Justice*.

Acknowledgements

My eternal thanks go to:
Amparo Dávila, Manuel Felguérez, Dr. Manuel Macías Patiño, Dr. Bernardo del Hoyo Calzada, Dr. Héctor Vega Carrillo, José Esquivel, Alfredo Valadez Rodríguez, Biblioteca de la Escuela de Minas de Zacatecas, Dr. Miguel Ángel Díaz Castorena, Eric Nava Muñoz, Fernando Salcedo, Daniel Garza Usabiaga, Willy Kautz, Gabriela Correa, Elizabeth del Ángel, Yolanda Segura, Sara Uribe, Mariana Oliver, Guillermo Espinosa Estrada, and Juan Pablo Anaya; this project would not have been possible without you all. Last but not least, to Christina MacSweeney and Cristina Rivera Garza. Also to Impronta Casa Editora and Sundial House for making an English home for *The Company*.

*The Company* was printed and bound in September 2024 in the Impronta Casa Editora workshops in Guadalajara, México. The interiors were offset printed on 120g Bond paper. The covers were letterpress printed on a Chandler 12 x 18 press on 300g Minagris paper. The first edition consists of 500 copies.